# I'M GLAD THERE ARE Bees and Other Bugs

By **Tracey Turner**     Illustrated by **Fiona Powers**

**W**
FRANKLIN WATTS
LONDON • SYDNEY

Franklin Watts
First published in Great Britain in 2022 by The Watts Publishing Group

Credits
Design and project management: Raspberry Books
Art Direction and cover design: Sidonie Beresford-Browne
Design: Kathryn Davies
Illustration: Fiona Powers

HB ISBN: 978 1 4451 8015 1
PB ISBN: 978 1 4451 8016 8

Printed in China

MIX
Paper from
responsible sources
FSC® C104740

Franklin Watts
An imprint of
Hachette Children's Group
Part of The Watts Publishing Group
Carmelite House
50 Victoria Embankment
London EC4Y 0DZ

An Hachette UK Company
www.hachette.co.uk

www.franklinwatts.co.uk

# I'M GLAD THERE ARE

# Bees and Other Bugs

By **Tracey Turner**     Illustrated by **Fiona Powers**

**W**

FRANKLIN WATTS

LONDON•SYDNEY

# Contents

Chirp

# I'M GLAD THERE ARE

# Bees and Other Bugs

**I LOVE BUGS!** They can be beautiful, like butterflies or brightly coloured beetles.

They can make a lovely sound, from the humming of a fuzzy bumblebee to the chirping of a cricket.

They can help our gardens grow. They are all amazing!

*Chirp*

IN THIS BOOK you will meet different kinds of insects – including bees, beetles and butterflies – and spiders. We're calling them all 'bugs', like lots of people do, but a bug is really a special kind of insect.

Bugs are right on your doorstep, waiting for you to visit them. Just look and listen.

**I'M GLAD THERE ARE**

# Bees

## ...because they're a sign that spring has come.

BEES start buzzing when the weather gets warmer and winter is over.

I like to watch bees as they fly from flower to flower, making their sleepy-sounding hum. There are lots of different kinds.

Bumblebees are the round, furry-looking ones.

Some kinds of bumblebee build their nests underground. Others nest in long grass, or in trees.

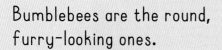

# An energy drink for a tired bee

If you see a bee on the ground that isn't moving much, mix up two teaspoons of sugar with one teaspoon of water on a small plate, and put it right next to the bee. You might see the bee take a drink to give it the energy to fly away.

SUGAR

I'M GLAD THERE ARE

# Honeybees

## ...because I love honey!

HONEYBEES buzz about collecting pollen and sucking up nectar from flowers. Back at their hive, they store the pollen for food, and use the nectar to make honey.

10

BEEKEEPERS keep bees in a hive, and take some of their honey for people to eat. They make sure the bees have enough for themselves.

By spreading pollen from one flower to another, bees help make seeds for new flowers. Lots of other bugs do this, too.

# Help a honeybee

We can help honeybees by planting the flowers they like – lavender is a honeybee favourite. You don't have to have a garden, because bees are just as happy to visit a windowbox!

HONEY

Lavender

Dahlias

# Ants

## ...because they are clever animals.

There are THOUSANDS of different kinds of ant. They live together in big groups called colonies.

As ANTS wander about looking for food, they leave a chemical trail behind them that other ants can follow.

Ants can carry many times their own weight. If you were like an ant, you could carry a grown-up with no problem at all.

Ants are clever. Some farm little bugs called aphids, protect them from predators, and drink the honeydew the aphids make!

Lots of ants live in tropical forests, like these leaf-cutter ants from Central and South America. They snip bits off leaves with their sharp jaws, carry them back to the ant nest, then use them to grow a special fungus, which is the ants' food!

I'M GLAD THERE ARE

# Butterflies

...because they are the most beautiful insects of all.

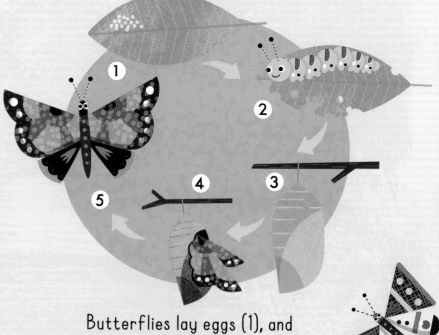

A BUTTERFLY'S brilliant colours can help it blend in with flowers, warn predators that it's not safe to eat, and attract other butterflies. The colours also make butterflies lovely to look at!

Butterfly young don't look at all like their parents.

Butterflies lay eggs (1), and caterpillars hatch from them (2). The caterpillar eats a lot, then turns into a pupa (3).

Then, inside the pupa, the butterfly grows and eventually comes out (4). When it's ready, it stretches out its wings and flies away (5). It's like magic!

## Butterfly bushes

If you have a garden, you could ask to plant a buddleia plant (or 'butterfly bush'), because butterflies love them. They have purple flowers and are easy to grow.

Buddleia

I'M GLAD THERE ARE

Chirp

Chirp

# Crickets

...because they make a lovely summer sound.

Most CRICKETS come out and start to make their chirping song after the sun goes down.

Crickets make the sound by rubbing their wings together – the top of one wing scrapes across the underneath of the other wing. Only male crickets make the noise, they do it to attract female crickets.

Chirp Chirp Chirp

Chirp Chirp Chirp

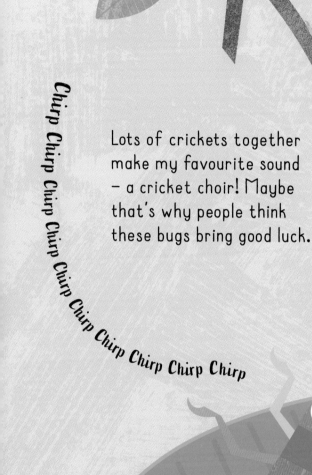

Chirp

Chirp Chirp Chirp Chirp Chirp Chirp Chirp Chirp Chirp Chirp Chirp

Lots of crickets together make my favourite sound – a cricket choir! Maybe that's why people think these bugs bring good luck.

# Make a bug hotel

To encourage crickets and all kinds of other bugs, make somewhere for them to shelter or lay their eggs. Use recycled plastic bottles with the front cut away and fill them with twigs, cardboard tubes, and dried-up flowers and leaves.

HOTEL

# Moths

## ...because they make the night-time magical.

Most MOTHS come out at night, or at dawn and dusk. Some sniff out scented flowers and drink their nectar – they have a long, thin tube to reach inside flowers. Some moths don't eat at all, and others eat carpets and clothes!

This beautiful atlas moth is one of the biggest kinds of moth in the world. Its wingspan can be 30 cm – the size of a dinner plate! It lives in Southeast Asia. It's one of the moths that doesn't eat, but spends its short lifetime finding a mate and laying eggs.

There are other insects that don't eat when they're adults. Their energy comes from the food they ate as larvae.

19

# Dragonflies

...because I love watching their acrobatic flight.

DRAGONFLIES are some of fastest flying insects, as they dart about hunting their prey. They can move backwards and sideways as well as forwards and up and down.

They have amazing bright colours. This one is a female emperor dragonfly.

Dragonflies often live near ponds because they lay their eggs in water. When they hatch, dragonfly larvae are fierce underwater predators before they become adult dragonflies.

# Peer into a pond

Ponds attract lots of other insects, too – damselflies (like small dragonflies), waterboatmen and lots more. Go pond watching with an adult and see how many bugs you can spot. You might see frogs and newts, too.

⚠ REMEMBER: always be careful near water!

# Beetles

## ...because they're incredible creatures.

There are hundreds of thousands of different types of BEETLE. If you made a list of all the different kinds of living things in the world, about one in every five would be some sort of beetle!

Ladybirds are beetles. They have two sets of wings – soft ones to fly, and hard ones like a shell that close over them. Most beetles have wings like this. I like the spots on a ladybird's hard outer wings.

Most beetles eat plants, but ladybirds eat smaller creatures. There are also creatures that eat them. If ladybirds think another animal is going to attack them, they can squirt poisonous chemicals from their legs!

Some beetles have gorgeous colours and patterns. Jewel beetles are shiny and come in bright colours, which confuses predators and makes the beetles harder for them to spot. This one is a multi-coloured beauty from Thailand.

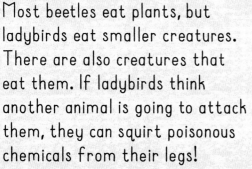

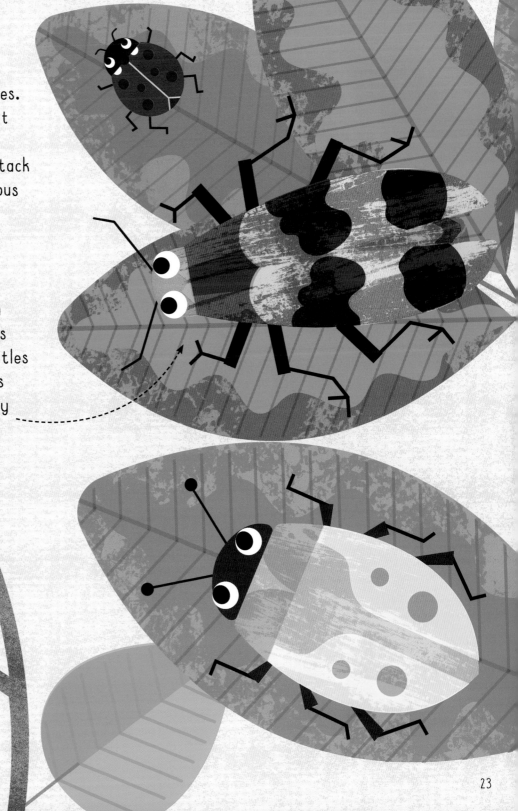

I'M GLAD THERE ARE

# Fireflies

## ...because they are like living fairy lights.

FIREFLIES twinkle on summer evenings using special light organs on their bodies. They flash on and off, just like lights on a Christmas tree.

Fireflies are a type of beetle. They light up the ends of their bodies to show one another where they are. There are about two thousand different kinds, and each kind has its own pattern of flashing lights!

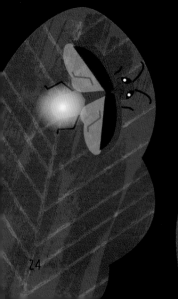

Fireflies spend most of their lives as larvae, which live underground feeding on slugs, snails and worms for up to two years. The larvae glow in the dark too! Adult fireflies usually only live for a few weeks.

# Spiders

## ...because I love their glittering webs.

**SPIDER WEBS** can look like strings of diamonds, especially early in the morning when the dew leaves tiny drops of water on the spider silk.

Spiders spin webs to catch smaller insects to eat.

A spider forms its web from silk made in 'spinnerets' on its body.

First the spider makes a bridge of silk from one place to another. Then it weaves the rest of the web – lines of silk to keep the web in place, spokes, like the spokes on a wheel, and a spiral from the middle to the outside.

All spiders can make silk, but not all of them make webs. Some pounce on their prey, and some live in burrows with trapdoors to surpise a small animal!

# Watch out for webs

Look out for spider webs and be careful not to break them! They take a lot of time and energy to make.

# I'M GLAD THERE ARE Pollinating Bugs

## ...because they make flowers grow!

BEES, BUTTERFLIES, HOVERFLIES, BEETLES and lots of other insects visit flowers and move pollen from one to another. This helps make seeds for new flowers.

Imagine a world without beautiful flowers! My favourites are bright orange marigolds.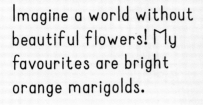

Some flowers turn into fruit and vegetables. So without pollinators we wouldn't have some delicious foods like raspberries, strawberries, peas and courgettes. Lots of the foods we eat need pollinators to help them grow.

# Pollinators in peril

Grow flowers to attract pollinators, but ask grown-ups never to spray plants with pesticides. Pesticides kill pollinators and other little creatures. Flowers don't need anything except water, sunshine and, sometimes, plant food.

# GLOSSARY

### Bug
a true bug is a particular kind of insect that has special mouth parts. People often call insects, spiders and other creepy crawlies 'bugs'.

### Caterpillar
a butterfly's larva is called a caterpillar.

### Chemical
our world is made up of different chemicals, which are substances that can't be broken down without changing them into something else.

### Fungus
one of a big group of living things that aren't plants or animals. Mushrooms, moulds and yeasts are all types of fungus.

### Insect
a small animal with six legs, three parts to its body (head, thorax and abdomen), and a hard outer shell called an exoskeleton.

### Larva
the wingless stage of an insect after it hatches from an egg and before it turns into an adult. More than one larva are called larvae.

**Nectar**
a sweet liquid made inside flowers to attract pollinators.

**Pollen**
the powdery substance that makes plants form seeds.

**Pollination**
when pollen is moved from one flower to another of the same type, the flower's egg cells are fertilized and make seeds, which eventually grow new flowers. Flowers are pollinated by the wind or by animals.

**Pollinator**
an animal that moves pollen from one flower to another. Animal pollinators include insects, birds and bats.

**Predator**
an animal that kills and eats other animals.

**Pupa**
some insects turn into a pupa, when they transform from a larva to an adult.

**Spider**
a small animal with eight legs and two parts to its body.

**Tropical forest**
a forest that grows in warm regions close to the equator, the imaginary line that runs around the middle of the world.

**Web**
a structure rather like a net that's made of thin threads of silk.

# INDEX

## TITLES IN THE SERIES:

| Bees and Other Bugs | Clouds and Rain | Humans and Other Animals | Oceans and Seas | Stars and the Moon | Trees and Other Plants |
| --- | --- | --- | --- | --- | --- |
| HB: 978 1 4451 8015 1 | HB: 978 1 4451 8048 9 | HB: 978 1 4451 8054 0 | HB: 978 1 4451 8052 6 | HB: 978 1 4451 8050 2 | HB: 978 1 4451 8046 5 |
| PB: 978 1 4451 8016 8 | PB: 978 1 4451 8049 6 | PB: 978 1 4451 8055 7 | PB: 978 1 4451 8053 3 | PB: 978 1 4451 8051 9 | PB: 978 1 4451 8047 2 |

# TITLES IN THE SERIES:

HB: 978 1 4451 8015 1
PB: 978 1 4451 8016 8

• Bees and Other Bugs • Bees
• Honeybees • Ants • Butterflies
• Crickets • Moths • Dragonflies
• Beetles • Fireflies • Spiders
• Pollinating Bugs

HB: 978 1 4451 8048 9
PB: 978 1 4451 8049 6

• Clouds and Rain • Different Types of
Cloud • Fluffy Clouds • Rain • Rainbows
• Sunshine • World Recycles Water
• Snow • Frost • Thunderstorms • Misty
Mornings • Seasons

HB: 978 1 4451 8054 0
PB: 978 1 4451 8055 7

• Humans • Dogs and Cats • Small Furry
Pets • Rainforest Animals • Polar Animals
• Insects • Grassland Animals • Sea
Creatures • Birds • Woodland Animals
• Monkeys and Apes • Australian Animals

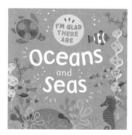

HB: 978 1 4451 8052 6
PB: 978 1 4451 8053 3

• Oceans and Seas • Beaches • Waves
• Tides • Whales and Dolphins • Coral
Reefs • Seabirds • Mangrove Swamps
• Ocean Zones • Estuaries • Deep-Sea
Creatures • Icy Seas

HB: 978 1 4451 8050 2
PB: 978 1 4451 8051 9

• Night Sky • Stars • Moon
• Sun • Eclipses • The Earth Is Tilted
• Solar System • Shooting Stars
• Asteroids • ISS • Astronauts
and Rockets • Galaxies

HB: 978 1 4451 8046 5
PB: 978 1 4451 8047 2

• Trees and Other Plants • Trees
• Trees for Birds • Deciduous Trees
• Evergreens • Flowers • Plants We
Can Eat • Desert Plants • Grasslands
• Forests • Rainforests • Houseplants

FRANKLIN
WATTS